THE WACKY WHACKING-OFF WORLD OF SEX

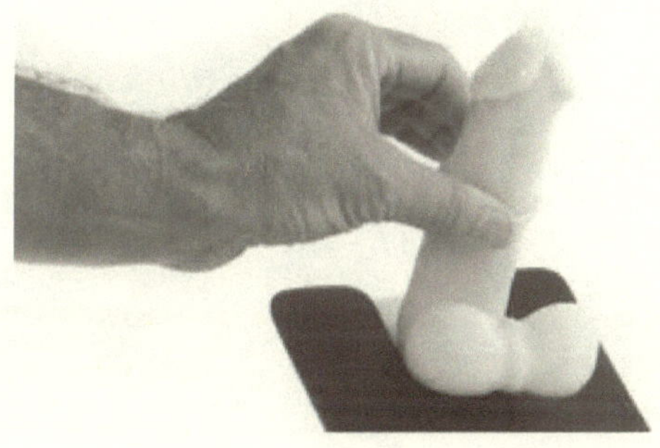

Naughty & Bawdy Antics

THE WACKY WHACKING-OFF WORLD OF SEX

Naughty & Bawdy Antics

by

ESMERALDA LINTNER

ϹƷ

Includes many illustrations and photos

This book is a work of fiction. References to real people, events, establishments, organizations or locales are intended only to provide a sense of authenticity and are used fictitiously. All other characters, incidents and dialogue are drawn from the author's imagination and are not to be construed as real.

Cover design provided by kdp.amazon
All illustrations and photos are in the public domain unless otherwise stated

ISBN 9798489265935
First printing December 2021

Printed in the United States of America

I dedicate this book so that one may enjoy the lighter side of sex. Use your erotic imagination as you enter into the funny world of naughtiness!

INTRODUCTION

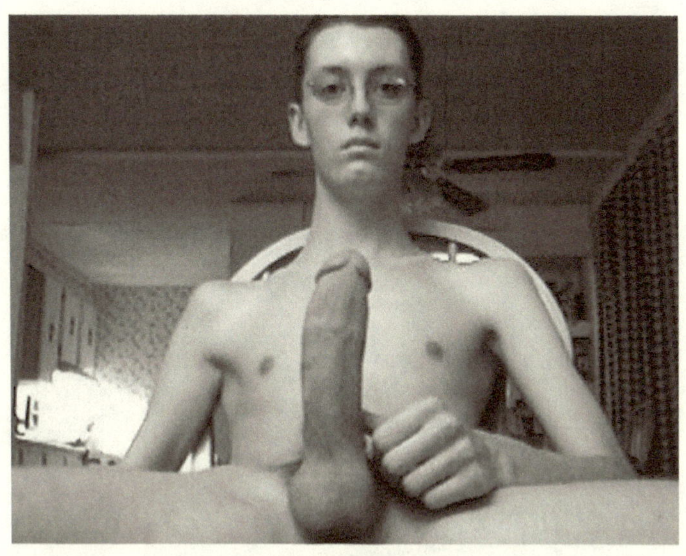

Have a hard time keeping it up?

Losing the old "oomph" to sexual satisfaction?

Like to reach that orgasmic, climactic state of colorful climax?

You've "cum" to the right place!

Join us now as you venture into the wacky whacking-off world of sex.

COMMERCIAL: **BONER-UP**

Having a hard time keeping the ol' wanker, wazoo of a wiener up?
Beating it off too much?
Going limp on you?
Trying to titillate the ol' pecker?
Now there's just the right resurrection for you!
Boner-Up:

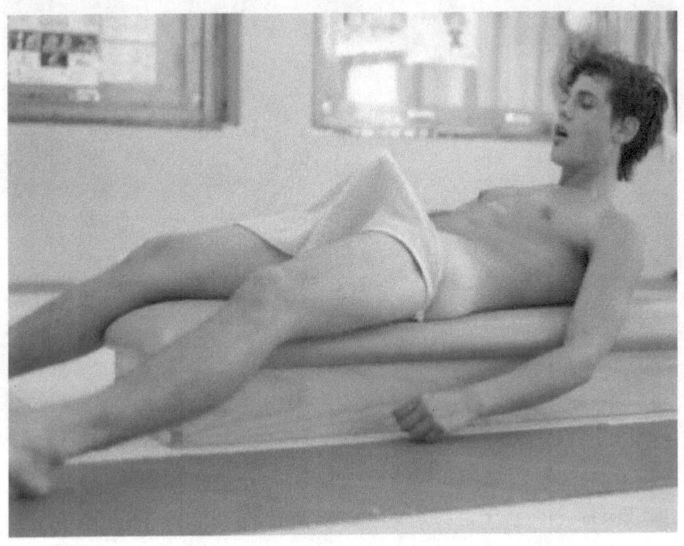

Just take one tablet daily and your cock will rise to new horizons.
For the biggest, long-lasting stiffie you've ever had, try it today!
Boner up, everyone!!

GAME SHOW: *BEAT THE COCK*

ANNOUNCER: Who will be the first to get it up?
Who will be the first to reach their hardest dong?
Who will beat theirs the fastest?
Find out who cums first!
You'll have a "hard" time watching.
See how our contestants give it all they've got.
Right here on "**BEAT THE COCK**."
Now here's your host, Bruce Betterhard!

HOST: Thanks, everybody, and welcome to another climactic release on "Bang the..." Oops, almost made a boo-boo there! I meant to say, "BEAT the Cock," everyone's favorite game show. Let's hit it off by meeting our two contestants and see which one can beat the old dong first.

ANNOUNCER: Bruce, from Cumington, West Virginia, meet Alex Assbeamer." (*applause*)

"And hailing from Ballerton University in Prickston, New Jersey, please welcome Dave Dickerson." (*more applause*)

Hi, you two! I hope you're both ready to show what you've got. I'll start with you, Dave. Tell me, how are things there at Ballerton University?

"We're doing great, Bruce. After every football game we gather in the locker room and give those balls a good healthy walloping. Yes indeed, sir, wherever and whenever we can get off, we do, especially at our frat parties. We beat our dicks 'til they go limp!"

I'll just bet you do. And how about you, Alex? How are things there in good ol' Cumington?

"Well, Bruce, we get together and do what every red-blooded American guy does: cum."

Good deal, Alex. That sound like a real "weiner."
(HOST unzips his pants, pulls his own dick out and elicits a huge laugh from the AUDIENCE. Stuffing it back into his pants, HOST continues)

Well, enough of that! Let's get on with our game, shall we? The rules are simple: the one who beats his cock into a frenzy and climaxes first is our winner. And would you let our contestants know what the winner receives as a prize, Mister Announcer?

"Bruce, our grand prize winner will receive a year's supply of 'Peckerhard' tablets, along with an additional year's supply of 'Miss Lydia Pinkum's Erotic Handsoap.' Miss Lydia Pinkum's soap will keep your jackoff hand sparkling fresh and clean after every jerk!"

Thanks, Mister Announcer, for enlightening us on those fantastic prizes, which are a rise in themselves. Now, let's see what the old wazoos will do as they perform. Whenever you're ready, gentlemen, whip 'em out!

(Both men do as instructed, showing their massive appendages to the HOST and AUDIENCES both in the studio as well as at home.)

Wow! Just look at them hammers, folks! Looks like you two've got big ones, for sure! You, Dave, have a slight edge over your opponent, Alex, who's an inch or two shorter, but still huge. Let's bring out the lube so our challengers can get right to it. Away we go!!

(AUDIENCE cheers wildly as the CONTESTANTS enthusiastically perform.)

Looks like our friend Dave from Ballerton University has a plump one. Oh, but Alex from

Cumington is trailing right behind him. Lots of stroking action is taking place, ladies and gentlemen. The clock on the old weiner wall is ticking away the minutes --- five already! And these amazing guys are still whacking away, can you believe it?! Gosh, Cumington, West Virginia is about to blow. Wow, what a gusher! A wanking good load if ever there was one. Our janitor'll have to get out here pronto to clean up this mess so nobody slips and falls accidentally. Congratulations, Alex Assbeamer from Cumington, West Virginia. Our winner of both year's supplies of fine Peckerhard and Lydia

Pinkum products. And so that you won't feel left out, Dave, we have a consolation prize: a free handjob --- and you get to pick the hand of your choice! How's that sound?

"Male or female, Bruce?"

Hey, man, whatever your little ol' cockeroonie desires, right?

That's all we have time for, friends. But don't forget to tune in to our next exciting installment of BEAT THE COCK. Bye for now!

COMMERCIAL: **EDNA'S**

Hi, girls! Are your dresses feeling too tight? And because of them, do you feel like shit? Whatever you do, girls, don't get your panties twisted out of shape. It's also not worth getting you titties in a tizzy.

Stop over at Edna's. I'm the Queen of all the drag queens. I'll lilly your lollies. I'm here for all your crossdressing needs. There's nothing Edna can't do. No she-male she can't dress! You'll be the tinsel of the town once I get through with you. I'll transform all you chauvinistic he-man into simpering lovely little ladies!

My secret is in my own secret sauce. I've got what it takes, Honey! Check out my pink and lavender laces. Notice my deep-dish chiffon dress. There's nothing too good for us crossdressers, you know. Once the boys get a load of you, they'll be popping their peckers in no time. Just see how sheer this dress is! Let me, Edna, make women out of you men.

Stop by my luscious boutique for all your crossdressing needs. And Happy Dressing to all of you out there!

YOUR EMAILS FOR THE PROFESSOR

Good day to you all. Allow me to introduce myself to you. I am Professor von Cummalingus-Titillacious the First. I am an expert on sexual performance. If you listen long enough to my lectures, you too can become cummalingus and titillacious yourself! I'll look forward to receiving your emails ad responding with my expert advice, whatever that's good for.

Here's an interesting one from Babs Babcock who hails from Butte, Montana: "I have a difficult time keeping my husband's cock aroused. Should I titillate, cumalingate or fellatiate?"

Well, Mrs. Babcock, you present an interesting problem, one that I've not read about before. My advice is: why not try all three? One or all of them should make your man go straight!

My next email comes from Joe Shaw who hails from Boonesville, Tennessee. Oddly enough, ole Joe writes the same way he talks: "Howdy there, how y'all doin'? I'm a direct descendant of the Chickawaw Indians. Recently I made love to the daughter of the Chickawaw chief, Old Rain-In-The-Puss. The only problem is that "me no want marry her." Somethin' went powerful wrong while we was makin' whoopee. Now that squaw has upped and is fixin' to have her a baby. Them Chickawaws have this strange custom 'bout naming their offspring somethin' colorful. Y'know, things like "Thunder Cloud," "Falling Rain" or "Wild Horse." But this li'l ol' papoose is gonna be born out o' wedlock. Chief Rain-In-The-Puss has jus' walked in while I'm typin' this here email to ya. He's got warpaint smeared all over his face, and he's holdin' a hatchet in his right han'. Frownin' and lookin' mighty displeased wit' me, he says, "You paleface, you in heap deep shit!" An' I says to th' Chief, "Well, what me do?" That's my question fer ya, Professor.

Well, Joe, something definitely went wrong. You might honor the Chief's and whole tribe's tradition by picking out a colorful name --- something like 'Broken Rubber,' for instance.

Another scintillating email comes from a Kansas City, Missouri lady named Martha Dobbs. And I have Martha here with me via the internet, talking live from her home out there. Good day, Martha, can you hear me?

"Yes, Professor, thank you. I'm eighty years old and still married to my husband who is ninety. This husband of mine complains about having a weak back every time we try to make love. I asked him, 'How long have you had a weak back, Lester?'

And you know what that dagburned varmint had the nerve to answer? 'Oh, about a week back!' Then he acted goofy and childish, going through all the motions he sees those wacky Three Stooges do in their short films.

"One afternoon, I came back from shopping at the Piggly Wiggly and caught him screwing with another woman. I went up the bed, rolled him over and kicked him in his nuts. Then I barked like a dog at his shackup floozy, somebody he refers to as 'Toots.' With my bare hands I picked up that scoundrel husband of mine and flung him across the bedroom. He flew right through the door and into a bathtub I'd filled with cold water to wash out some colored laundry. It occurred to me that what I'd just accomplished with that mangy brute was a "flying fuck." I was so tickled, I just stood there laughing myself to death.

Good for you, Martha. That'll teach that cheating husband of yours a thing or two. As the old saying goes, "If they can fuck at that age, they can fly!"

THE GENTILE/SEMITIC COMEDY HOUR

(excerpt from an upcoming show)

A young married couple spent their first night together. Unfortunately they had both been brought up with strict religious backgrounds. One belonged to a fundamentalist Christian church, while the other was a holy roller Jew. Man, what a weird combination that was!

Mary, tender and shy, slipped into bed wearing a flimsy nightgown. Johnathan entered into bed clad in his yarmulke and prayer shawl. His faithful wife lay patiently waiting for him. Mary pulled back the bedsheets and removed her nightgown. She took a Bible from the nightstand and placed it over her "privates." Johnathan began wailing and chanting Hebrew prayers.

"Good Lord," Mary exclaimed, "my Bible just fell to the floor. At the same time my vagina is going 'open --- close, open --- close.'"

"That's nothing to be concerned about, Bubeleh," Johnathan reassured her. "Your snatch is merely talking in tongues."

"Is it really? What is it saying?"

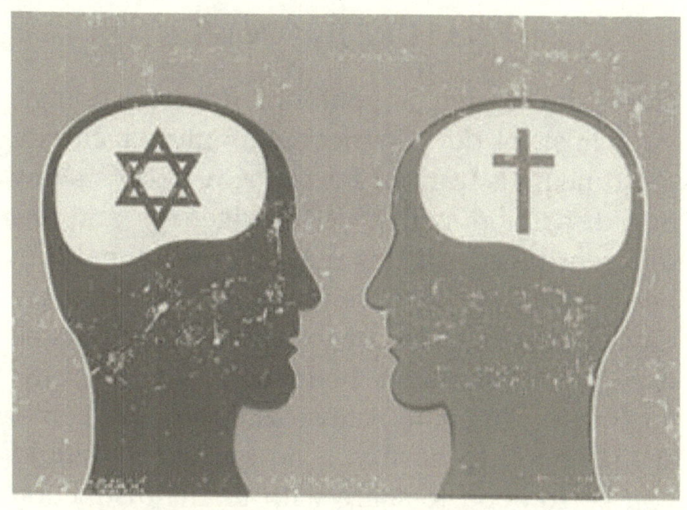

"Be fruitful and multiply," the Jewish husband replied, "enter into the joy of the Lord."

Scratching her head, Mary thought for a few seconds, then blurted out, "Oh, I get it. You mean let's fuck."

Johnathan smiled and shouted, "Give me a big 'amen' and a 'hallelujah.' Oy vey, I'll make certain this screw is kosher."

NATURE IN FOCUS

Good day to all of you! I'm Robert Jennings, your host for our afternoon show to which you are tuned, "Nature in Focus." On today's show our discussion will be on hedgehogs and the different breeds of this magnificent animal. I'm here at the San Diego Zoo on this glorious sunny day. And it is an honor to have with me a true expert on "all things hedgehog," as they say: zoologist Christian Schwanzfahrter. Welcome, sir, it's good to have you on our show. Would you be so good to share with us the distinction in the hedgehog family?

"Jawohl, I vould be heppie to do zo, Herr Jennings. If you komm mit me zis vey, you vill see zat ve hevv on ze left hennd zide ze African hedgehog, und on ze right hennd zide iss ze Nord American hedgehog."

"I see. But tell me, how you can tell one hedghog from the other?"

"As you kenn zee, ze African hedgehog hez ze twelve-inch prick, und ze Nord American hedgehog hez ze ten-inch prick."

"My goodness, Mister Schwanzenfahrter, you must realize this is a family-oriented show. We can't have you mixing up words. Surely there is some misunderstanding. You must mean the quill, if I am not mistaken.

"Ach ja, ze kvill. You're right, Herr Jennings. Ja, I believe ze pricks are about ze same size!"

BOOK OF FAIRY TALES

Now it's time for a story from our wacky, wanking Book of Fairy Tales. There once was a man who lived during the Roaring Twenties. The poor guy just loved to drink and ended up sleeping his life away. He was tired of all the noise of the big city, so he moved to the countryside, deep in the woods of Old Kentucky. He hired a construction company to build a nice log cabin.

"This is the perfect place for me to finally get some peace and quiet," he thought to himself. One morning he decided to venture out into the woods, for he loved Mother Nature. As he walked through the woods and slowly wore himself out, he decided to lie down beside an old log, resting his head. A beautiful oak tree spread out above him. "I'll just rest a spell, maybe even take a little nap here where it's so peaceful," he said to himself.

Falling fast asleep after a short time, his slumber was sound. Suddenly he felt a hand touch him. He awoke, rubbed his eyes and saw a young boy with his dog. "Are ya alright, Mister?" the boy asked. The man shook himself and tried to stand up, but he couldn't make it. Something pulled him down, and he couldn't

figure out for the life of him what it was. Looking down at the struggling man, the boy's eyes grew bigger and he cowered in fright. "Lordy me," he said, "that ol' pecker o' yours is the biggest I ever did see. Must be a mile or more long, Mister."

Surprised and perplexed, the man shot back, "I'm confused, sonny. I was just walking along, got tuckered out and decided to lie down and rest my head on this log for a spell. Then I was fixin' to return to my cabin over yonder."

"A cabin over yonder?" the boy asked. "There ain't no cabins 'round these parts. They took 'em all down years ago. They plowed 'em over to make room for one of them new fandangled shoppin' centers. They put in a Walmart, Piggly-Wiggly, CVS and one o' them dang Starbucks coffee places. Right next to them you can take your cellphone in to get boosted or repaired."

"Cellphone? Walmart? Good Lord, child, I'm afraid I don't understand what you're saying. The last thing I recall was moving from Chicago where all the speakeasies were. Al Capone and his gang were tearin' up the town then."

The boy blinked and looked intently at the man. "You must be livin' in the past, sir. This here's the year 2021."

Glancing around and then taking account of his own being, the man exclaimed, "The funny thing is I don't look any older and haven't changed a bit. The only difference about me in this enormous cock. And that's just when it's soft, too."

Laughing, the boy asserted, "I wager y'all can make a shitload o' babies with that long dong o' yours, Mister. But what's all this here talk about speakeasies and Al Capone?"

"The only thing I can make of it, son," the man began, "is that I fell asleep and woke up a little less than a hundred years later."

"Golly," the kid said, "if that's true, you'll be famous. You'll be known for the biggest dick in town, maybe the whole world." Scratching his head and thinking, he added, "I got me an idea. I'll call you Chip Van Tinkle, the man who slept a hundred years and woke up with a mile-long prick."

Remember, dear friends, if you ever happen to be out for a stroll and come upon a wide river flowing with a tidal wave of yellow water, there you will find the longest, wankiest wanker-weiner of the world.

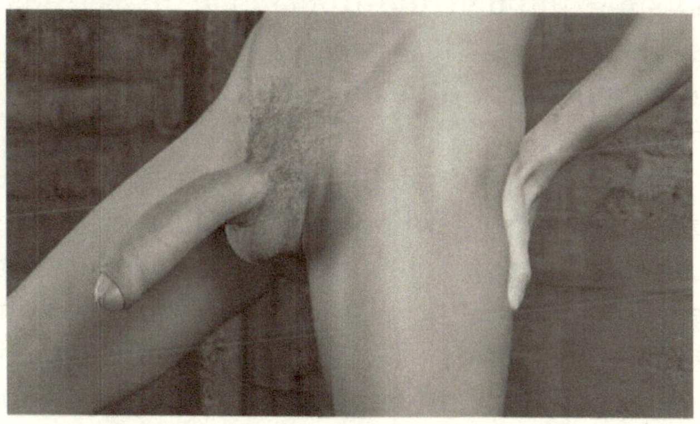

YELLOW BALLS

A well-dressed gentleman in his thirties tied up his little Chihuahua puppy outside his favorite coffee and bagel shop. After about twenty minutes the man slipped back outside to check on his dog. He stepped back in fright and covered his mouth.

"Chico!" he shouted. "Who the hell painted your balls yellow?" Upset, he stumbled across the street and pushed through the double-doors of a bar he happened to see, looking for troublemakers. What he didn't know was that this was the leading lesbian hangout in town. Bursting through the front door, he screamed like a banshee. "Listen up! I wanna know who here painted my little dog's balls yellow!"

Ignoring him totally, the women gathered around the bar and seated at tables continued drinking away. Frustrated with their lack of reaction, the angry man stomped his feet and clapped his hands. "Hey, you dykes! Listen, and listen good! One of you painted my little Chico's balls yellow, and I'm gonna find out who the culprit is."

A very butch-looking woman wearing tight blue jeans and covered in tattoos approached

him, got into the man's face and sneered, painted the mutt's balls yellow, Buster. Wanna make somethin' of it?"

Cringing in fear, the man smiled reluctantly and responded, "You might like to know, Lady, that the first coat is dry.

TITTY TATTOOS

A girl in her late twenties with flaming orange bushy hair and a pierced ring on her nose speaks in a commercial: "Hi, gang! Would you love to have tattoos put on your body? Have you thought of titillating your tits and nipples even more? Why not stop on by and try out my special 'Titty Tattoos'? Not only will you get a great feeling, but you can also show off your

lovely titties as well. You'll drive men crazy. They'll just love tasting those titillating titties of yours. We have piercings as well. You men might want those plump heads of yours pierced to show yourselves off better. Be sexy, be smart. Show off your tits and give the horny toads around your town all you've got. Come one, come all to Tina's Tattoo Parlor. First time customers receive a complimentary cock-tease piercing. So why not stop on by and give your titillating titties the attention they deserve?" Waving enthusiastically, she closes by saying, "Happy Titty Time to all you out there!"

COMMERCIAL: **GLADIATOR CONDOMS**

The Trojan Horse appears and a group of warriors jump out from its base. They are girded for battle.

A muscular soldier emerges from the crowd, addressing his fellow soldiers solemnly: "Are any of you in need of good, strong protection for that pride and joy hanging between those legs of yours? Does it need that extra stretch when tugging and pulling? For cock-pleasing protection, slip this on and start sliding down the old shaft."

Fingering a limp, unlubricated transparent condom, he continues, "There's nothing like the tough, durable fit of a *Gladiator*. Using just one of these cute little goodies'll make a real warrior out of you. Helmet up for that glorious peckerhead of yours. Durable and long-lasting, it suffices for every kind of humping and whacking action you can give it.

Do like all us warriors do: try GLADIATOR CONDOMS. It'll make your cock a true warrior.

(we join a show already in progress due to an earlier pre-emption of the big game)

Now it's time for the **WACKY WHACKING-OFF TALENT HOUR**. Let's welcome the Oversexed Quartet."

As the announcer completes his introduction, four nude boys come onstage, each sporting a straw hat and a cane like the minstrels of old. The first boy steps forward and asks, "Isn't it fun to beat your meat?"

Then he begins a song and dance routine with the other three, frolicking round the stage.

"Isn't it a real treat to beat your beat?"
they chirp.
"It's so chic
to stroke that meat.
Grab that stroking shaft
and give it a beat.
A beat to
your meaty-meat."

The chorus croons, "Oh, how we love to!"

Then all four belt out the final line of their routine:

"Oh, how we love to beat
that wonderful, handsome,
sexy meat!
Try it!
It's so sweet andoh! so neat
to beat your meat.
Just love to stroke it.
Beat that meat!"

With a final, breathily-enounced, "Yeah….!", the four naked lads shuffle off the stage.

VENTRILOQUIST

Now it's time for *Peter and His Talking Peckerhead.* A ventriloquist appears, carrying his dummy which resembles the head of a penis.

"Hey there, Peckerhead, how's it goin'?"

"Oh, fine," the dummy replies nonchalantly, "Hard-up as ever. Or, should I say, I'm as hard as ever."

"And what'cha been up to?"

"I've been tryin' on my new suit."

"Really?" the stunned ventriloquist exclaims. "I never knew you wore suits."

"Yeah, sure. It's made of snug, tight elastic. Them condoms'll fit me every time, 'specially when I get myself all lubricated and goosed up."

"You don't say! Goosed-up, huh? Why's that?"

"It looks like I'm not the only dummy round here. Everyone knows you need a good goosing now and then. By the way, Mister Dummy Man, did I tell ya I love the flavors them condom

manufacturers have been puttin' out lately? Why, there's strawberry, cherry and blackberry. If I had my way, I'd come up with one called 'cumberry,' y'know. I could blow my mind AND make my eyes pop out at the same time. Thar she blows! Just call me 'The One and Only Dickhead.' Just can't get enough o' that sucker-pucker power. No way, though, do I wanna catch anything from anybody, y'know, like sores on the mouth or pimples on the ass. That's all I'd need is to catch it and pass it on, for chrissakes."

"So Peckerhead," the ventriloquist asks, "please explain exactly what you've been doing with yourself."

"Just so happens," the dummy quips, "that I've been out in nature --- y'know, 'mong the birds 'n the bees. Kept busy practicin' my bird calls."

"Can you give us an example?"

Clearing his throat, the Peckhead shouts, "Cock-a-doodle do! Any-cock'll-do! As a matter of fact, Mister Ventriloquist, I also love poetry. You might say I'm one o' them educated pricks."

"Since time is so short, Dummy," the ventriloquist says, "maybe you'd better illuminate us with one of your poetic gems before we pack up for the day."

"Sure,Bubbie, anything for you. Here goes:

Peter Piper
pricked his
pickled pecker.
And if he pickled
any more peckers,
then how many would he have?
A bushel and a
peck o' pickled peckers.

NOW THAT'S ITALIAN!

Two Italians went into their favorite restaurant. Both reminisced about their sex lives as they ate delicious pasta.

"Hey, Angelo," Michael said in between mouthfuls, "they don't call me the hottest stud in Brooklyn for nut'in'. I can keep my dick hard for hours, bangin' one broad after another. I've fucked every dame in this town 'ceptin' my sister and my muddah."

His buddy looked at him in disbelief. "*Mamma mia*," he cried, "that's a hot one. I guess between the two of us we've fucked 'em all, huh?"

Angelo put down his silverware, rose abruptly from his chair and sailed across the table, grabbing his "friend" by the neck and strangling him.

YOUR FAVORITE GERMAN LADY

Now it's time for our very favorite German lady, Frau Gretl Goosen Scheckelgruben. Ladies and Gentlemen, you see this elderly woman here with the glasses falling off her nose, but she is ready to address all of you out there in TV Land:

"*Guten Morgen,* meine Herren and Heeresses. I am your expert of all things sexual. Today I shall endeavor to explain to you what we affectionately refer to in German as 'ze birds und ze bees.' I always say that if you don't watch yourself, you may get your asses schtung. Ach, how my boobies just love bouncing up and down to the beat of the oomp-pah-pah music. It looks like my nipples are sunny side up.

"Today, as you can see, I shall place here on this table a replica of what we call back in the Old Country, 'ze cockens und ze ballens.' *Ach du lieber,* this particular one is a sizeable *Schwanzen*-pickle. With one of these it's easy to tickle the erogenous zones.

"In addition to the cockens and ballens, we have what I like to refer to as 'ze pussy.' When you put these two things together, the result is always one enormous schtup. That's why we sometimes need birth control to avoid the obvious, and for this we employ the condom or, as *Grossmutter* use to say, 'don't go out without your rubbers.' This applies in particular to all you young men out there who are subjected to the *Schwanzen*-boner.

"You know, , all this talk about schtupping has got me hot; I could use a good one right about now. This is a good time to illustrate the various positions: the missionary style, the traditional way of fucking, as well as 'doggy style,' which you can use your imagination to figure out what it means.

"*Donnerwetter,* I see we have appearing out of nowhere a handsome naked man. 'What are you doing, you horny young stud? How dare you throw me on this table and start to mount me! My poor heart can't take these palpitations. This activity is much too nefarious for me, you cad.'

As the young man penetrates me without stopping, I beg him, 'Oooh, please don't schtop! Do some more!' You'll have to excuse me, ladies and gentlemen of our viewing audience, but I have some important matters to attend to at the moment. I leave you with these appropriate words: Happy Schtupping to All, and to all a good night!"

INFOMERCIAL: **JERK-A-BONER**

Do you suffer the embarrassment of a small cock? Tired of being made fun of in the lockroom of your high school or college? Let's peek in on this group of boys taunting a poor fellow student of theirs who happens to have a tiny penis. There's plenty of snickering and lewd comments going on.

"Man, that sure looks like a little wiener that never made it."

"If he tried to screw some girl, he'd barely get a squirt out o' that puny thing."

Another hapless young man on a hot date with his sweetheart slithers into the backseat of his roadster with her and unzips his pants. The girl whose name is Mary glances at the poor guy's miniscule member and winces. "Sorry, Johnny, I don't think so. Your weewee's not good enough for me."

"It ain't no weewee. It's a prick. Whatsa matter wit' it anyhoo?"

Grinning, Mary replies, "I've seen lots o' pricks in my time, Buster, and yours is definitely a weewee."

If only these guys had found out about our great new product, *Jerk-a-Boner*! Two cock-growing capsules daily in conjunction with a complimentary set of vibrating lips or hands (your choice when you order!) are guaranteed to produce a hammer that will continue to grow and grow forever. Within hours you'll be sporting an impressive ten to twelve inch prick.

"The bigger, the better," as the old saying goes, isn't that right, gentlemen? No doubt about it: you'll be the talk of the town. Nobody'll ever poke fun at you anymore, because you'll be able to poke them back!

"Wow, what a massive cock that guy has! He can satisfy any dame that comes along."

And little ol' Mary'll come back to new, revived and improved Johnny with unbridled enthusiasm: "Gee, Johnny, you're so big! You might bust me wide open with that huge thing. Eeeek!"

So be sure to run out and buy yourself the all-new *Jerk-A-Boner*. It's available everywhere when fine sex aids are sold.

JACK-O, THE JACK-OFF CLOWN

And now it's time for Jack-o, the Jack-off Clown.

"Hey, everybody! It's great to be back again. There's nothing like a good jacking off to start you on the right path. It's time to stroke it, all you lovely viewers out there in television land. Come and join me along with our friend and my bosom buddy, Humpy-Humpy."

"Gee, Jack-o, it's great to be here. I just finished me off a big platter o' fried eggs at the local diner located around the corner from our studio."

"Oh, that's very interesting, Humpy ol' boy. You might say it's egg-citing to have you here today!"

"Yeah, real egg-citin'!"

"So how are you anyway, Humpy? How's tricks?"

"I had an accident early this morning. I fell off the wall and landed on my balls."

"Aw, too bad. What a rotten break for ya."

"Yeah, I won't be able to humpy-humpy anymore and live up to my name."

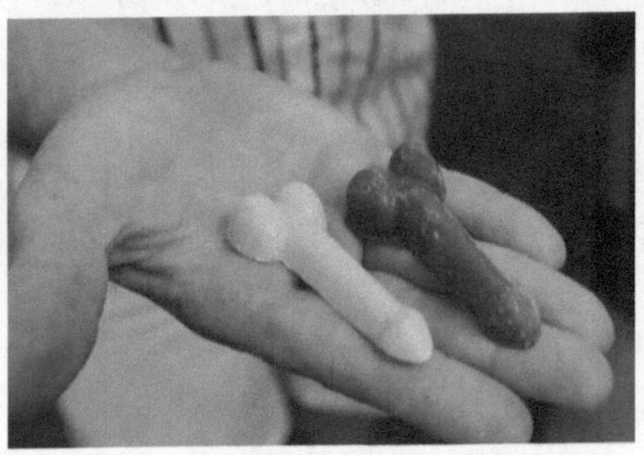

"Hey, I've got a swell idea. Why don't you try my new *Jack-o Chocolate Flavored Cock*? You'll be good and hard in no time after just a few healthy bites. I've got 'em with and without nuts, if you'll pardon the expression. The one thing I don't skimp on is the delicious cum-filled center. You wanna try one, Humpy?"

"Don't mind if I do, Jack-o. Hmm..., Delicious! I'll be back humpy-humping in no time."

"So do like Humpy and grab yourself of bunch of my new *Jack-o Chocolate Flavored Cocks*. If you don't happen to like chocolate, I've invented a dozen other flavors, including strawberry, vanilla and caramel cappuccino swirl, just to name a few."

"Remember what my buddy Jack-o always says: 'A cock-a-day'll keep ya humpin' long after.'"

"Thanks a bunch, Humpy ol' sport. Now, ladies and gentlemen, boys and girls, it's time for the Jack-o the Jack-off Clown Pledge: 'I promise to keep my wiener-wanger healthy and happy every day and in every way.' And now it's time to say good-bye. I leave you with these words: keep the ol' wanker wanking off, whatever you do. I'll just revv up the old Jack-o Jack-offmobile and head for the hills! Our choir will sing our lovely theme song for you:

I love to do it
I love to stroke it
There's nothing like
Fondling and fiddling
My twiddle-dee-dee.
If you don't be careful
You'll grow hair on your hands
Let's do it
Just you and me.
C'mon, let's go
To another X-rated show.
Stroke it, stroke it,
Same time, new show,
Let's blow,
Here we go.

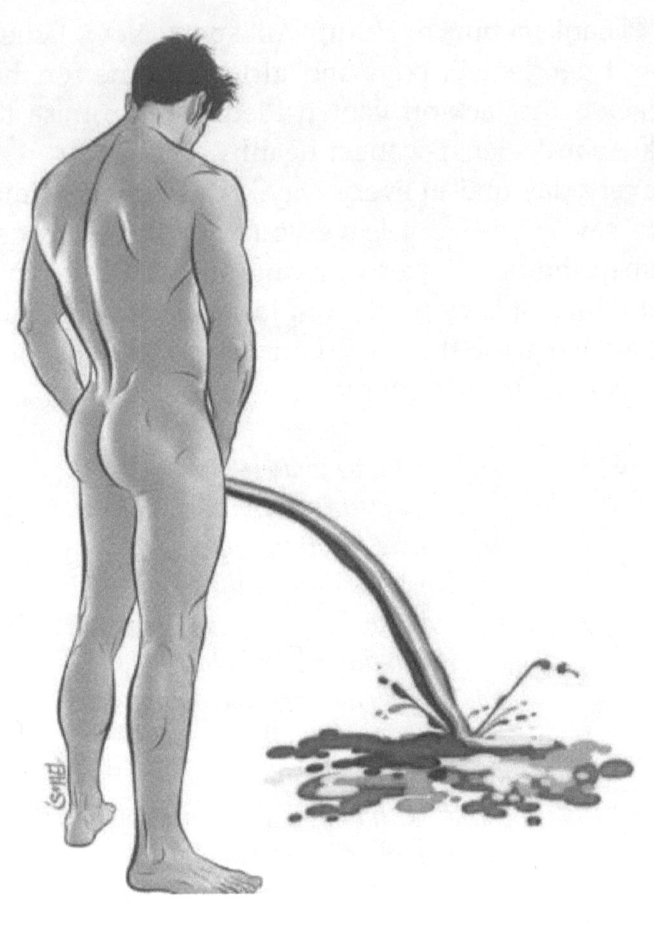

THE SIDEWALKS OF NEW YORK

(A typical sidewalk in the heart of New York City. A man stands there with his young son and the son's girlfriend. Another man approaches the father. The girl waves.)

"Hi, Daddy! How're ya doin'?" Pointing to her boyfriend and the boy's father, she adds, "You already know Mister Shaunessey and Johnny, huh?"

Scowling, the father says, "Yeah, I know 'em. Listen here, Shaunessey, if I ever get my hands on that screwy kid o' yours," the second man says threateningly, "I'll strangle 'im."

Taken aback, the father replies, "What could he possibly have done to make you all upset like this?"

"I'll tell ya what he did," Man Number Two sneers. "Your little asshole of a son jacked off with his name all over the sidewalk."

"Big deal!" Man Number One shoots back. "So whadyou care if he does it?"

"I'll tell you why, wiseguy," the irate man snorts. "Because it's in my daughter's handwriting."

SUPERDICK

Here's comes another exciting adventure your way with the one and only SuperDick! He is a mild-mannered park pervert who delights in exposing himself while streaking in public. Watch out, for the super-headed dick is headed your way! SuperDick has super-squirting and super-cumming powers. With his anti-gravity balls SuperDick is able to fly where no dick has flown before. Let's join our park pervert as he strolls across the rose garden while clearly exposing himself to one and all…

"Howd'ya like this package?" he proudly proclaims. His super peckerhead radio transmitter suddenly vibrates. "Hmm… That always makes my ol' wiener throb. Can't get enough!"

He listens attentively and recoils in horror. "Jeesh, Holy Cock and Balls! I just heard headquarters inform me that a burglary's taken place at the local bathhouse and adjoining lockerroom. It looks like another job," he juts out his chest and wiggles his member, "for SuperDick! I'll give them crooks a hard time when they get a healthy slap of my dick power."

Prior to SuperDick's arrival, clients of the bathhouse are being held up at gunpoint. "Stick 'em up, all you humpers!" one of the burglars snarls. Little do the robbers know that SuperDick is about to burst on the scene, utilizing his magic dickhead powers to the max.

"OK, you crumb bums," our hero yells as he flies into the scene of the crime. "Take this!" Pulling out his adhesive cum-gun from between his balls, he aims it at the criminals. One of them writhes in pain and falls on the ground as he is overhelmed by the sticky goo shooting out of the cum-gun. A second crook is subjected to a similar sticky mess and squirms in agony.

SuperDick sees the results of his cum-gun operation and bursts out laughing. "It looks like we've got a bunch of stuck-up fellas here." Our hero smiles at the bathhouse clients, takes a flying leap and shoots up into the sky. "Up, up and away!" he shouts as he slowly disappears.

COMMERCIAL: DOGGIE DONGS DONUTS

Are you an animal lover? Do you like having your pet follow you wherever you go?

Now you can enjoy your special dog AND pleasure yourself with your own wagging, wanking dong. Why not take a bite out of the ol' dong?

Try our delicious DOGGIE DONGS, shaped like a real bowser dong. They come in an assortment of mouthwatering glazes: chocolate, French vanilla, caramel, and our latest: doggy-cum-filled custard.

So wag your tail on down. Visit us wearing your Doggy Dong collar and you'll receive a complimentary free battery-operated doggy dong. It's great to bring to parties!

Be sure to stop by, all you woofers out there, and sink your choppers into a delicious Doggy Dong!

THE IMPECCABLE MISTER WANG

Now it's time for the Wacky, Wanking World of Sex premier movie. *The Impeccable Mister Wang,* accompanied by his illustrious son, Wun Hung Wang.

Our story takes place in an abandoned fortune cookie factory. "Ah, Number One Son," the Impeccable Mister Wang exclaims, "I have another exciting cookie to crumble."

"What is it, Honorable Father?" Wun Hung Wang asks obediently.

"You speak to me in a respectful tone and make me proud, son. You are descended from a long line of Wangs." Glancing up and down at his boy, he adds, "I can see that you are also very gifted."

"That's right, Honorable Father," the son replies. "They don't call me Wun Hung Wang for nothing. What's the case, Pops?"

"We must stop the mysterious Doctor Screw."

"Screw? Can you elaborate, Dad?"

"What a dumb cluck you are, Sonny Boy," the

Impeccable Mister Wang quips. "Cluck rhymes with fuck. You need many lessons about the birds and bees, my boy. Doctor Screw and his deadly screw machine must be stopped at all costs. Just one shot from that evil machine and the poor sap who receives the bullet will screw himself to death."

"Oh, I get it, Pop," the son says, scratching his head. "You mean, as in 'permanently screwed.'"

"Finally," the older man shoots back, throwing up his hands, "I see that something has registered in that soggy eggroll brain of yours."

Squirming, the boy responds, "I'm trying, Honorable Father. You don't have to get all mushy about it."

"Doctor Screw's overwhelming presence was last felt during the recent Family Values Convention, held at the Redd Foxx Hotel and Casino in beautiful downtown Reno, Nevada. Well-respected leaders of government and the Moral Majority were overcome by shots from the wicked doctor's contraption. Over fifty percent of them screwed themselves to death. It ruined a lot of lives, especially those who were in the throes of extramarital or same-sex liaisons."

"Holy Confucius, Father," the son cries in anguish. "It sounds as if they can't keep their dick-dongers to themselves."

"What a wise cookie you are, Son," the old man says proudly.

"Correction, Dad. You mean 'fortune cookie,' right?"

Slapping the young man's wrist, Mister Wang retorts, "I'll tell the jokes around here, Sonny Boy. Let's head over to the Redd Foxx Casino at once."

"Oh, goody-goody-goody!" Wun Hung Wang shouts. "I just love playing those slots."

Displeased, Mister Wang scolds him. "Screw first --- slots later!" Within minutes they arrive at the red-carpeted entrance of their destination.

Dozens of people staying on the fourteen floors of the adjoining hotel are buck naked and lolling around in their beds. The dead among them are carried out on stretchers by the emergency medical team. Father and Son survey the scene and recognize a few faces.

"Get a load of that one, Father," Wun Hung Wang whispers. "Isn't he the Megachristian Church pastor who's always preaching against sin and licentiousness on television?"

"Regrettably yes, Son. You are much more perceptive than I give you credit for. You are finally using your great Wang insight."

"Someone who worked at the fortune cookie factory told me through the grapevine that the gentleman was blessed with an enormous package."

"Very observant, My Brilliant Son. If you become any more intelligent, you will be dangerous.Number One Son, come here."

"Be right with you, Dad. I'm chomping at the bit to play them slots."

"Wun Hung Wang," the old man scolds, "you have a one-track mind. I see a trail of tire tracks leaving this area."

“True, Father,” the young man observes. “I noticed that lots of animals around here are making love to each other. Even the toads are getting in on, hot and heavy. You can say they’re really a bunch of horny toads.”

Mister Wang glances at his son with displeasure. “That was pretty lame, my boy. Let’s get going already. This horny trail will surely lead us to the criminals’ hideout.”

So the Impeccable Mister Wang in the company of his illustrious son are hot on the trail of the mysterious Doctor Screw. The trail goes on for quite a few miles, then abruptly ends.

“Hmm,” Mister Wang strokes his chin, “it appears that the trail ends at this enormous dildo factory.”

“Right-o, Honorable Father,” Wun Hung Wang exclaims. “It is said that many an exceptional cock has been created within these walls.”

Puzzled, the father turns to his son and asks, “How do you come by this information?”

Blushing, Wun Hung Wang declares, “I’ve sampled a few of them in my time. The doubleheaded doozy is my all-time favorite.”

"Doubleheaded doozy? You've got to be joking, son."

"Not at all, Honorable Father. You know what they say: 'two heads are better than one.'"

Clearing his throat, Mister Wang brings them back to the case at hand. "Let's forget about that right now and focus our attention on where the tracks leave off. It looks like the door to that factory is slightly ajar. Mighty suspicious, if you ask me."

"Honorable Father," the son says, bowing, "the depth of your wisdom is never-ending."

Smiling, the older man quips, "Aw shucks, tell me more."

Turning to the viewing audience, the son cups his hand and murmurs, "It looks like the old man's getting a big head." Then facing his father once again, he adds, "There's a light on right inside of that open door. I hear moaning and groaning. Maybe Doctor Screw is closer than we think."

Sure enough, the evil doctor is inside, sitting at a huge desk and gloating while fingering an impressive flesh-colored latex dildo. A group of admirers surround him. "I shall rule the world with my new invention." His attention diverted, he cries, "What's that noise? Go see who it is. I have the feeling we have uninvited guests."

Doctor Screw's goons drag the Impeccable Mister Wang and Wun Hung Wang to the chamber where Doctor Screw sits in all of his splendor. "Shit," he snarls, "it's that chow-mein teriyaki-basted Wang and his fortune cookie-headed son. That kid's as big as a tortoise with a hard-on."

Mister Wang, Wun Hung Wang and Doctor Screw stare at one another menacingly. "Your screwing days are over, dear Doctor," the old man shouts.

"That's what you think, you reject from a chop suey factory." Doctor Screw reaches into a desk drawer and pulls out a horny gun, firing several shots. Each time he entirely misses hitting either Mister Wang or his son. Instead, bullets from the horny gun hit a display of dildos. The inaminate objects suddenly take on life of their own, coming alive with devilish smiles on their faces. They sprout swift little legs, jump from the shelves and begin pursuing Doctor Screw around the room.

"Help, help!" the hapless man screams. "I'm being attacked by my own horny dildos. Argggghhhh!"

Wun Hung Wang turns to his father and says proudly, "Looks like you've wrapped up another case, Dad."

Modestly, Mister Wang holds up an instructive finger and replies, "Indeed, my son. It looks as if Doctor Screw learned his lesson, having been screwed by his own creation."

"I guess from here on out it won't be far-fetched to tell Doctor Screw to go fuck himself."

"You come from a long line of Wangs," the father proclaims, "with a perceptive, keen and cunning mind."

And so we leave the Impeccable Mister Wang and his obedient son Wun Hung Wang and urge you not to miss the next exciting cookie-crumbling episode!

THE GOOD DOCTOR

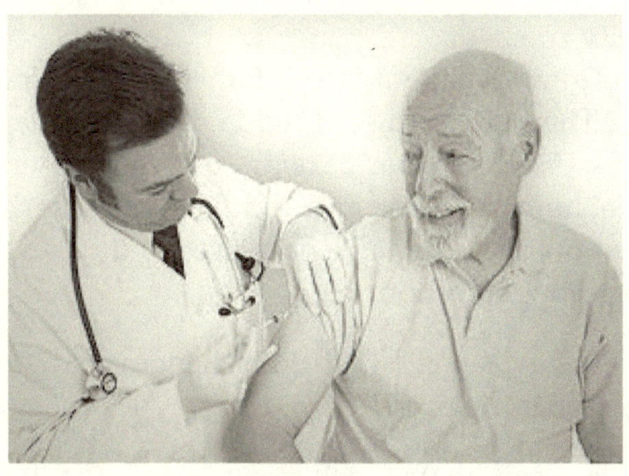

A doctor's office.
The good doctor is administering penicillin shots for venereal disease to a line of patients;

a priest with folded hands,
a rabbi whose head is covered with a prayer shawl,
a man in an angel's costume,
a Muslim imam who bows reverently toward Mecca are at the front of the line.

Shaking his head, the doctor laments,
"Why does this always have to happen to the nice guys?"

SPOILED

A city zoo.
Two giraffes take a stroll: father and his infant son. They pause to eat food laid out in different areas. As they chomp away, they are observed by a human father and toddler boy. The little boy points to the enclosure and asks an interesting question.

"Daddy, what's that thing hanging down on the big giraffe papa?"

"We call that a penis, my son," the father answers solemnly. "Why do you ask?"

"Because when I came here last time and looked at the giraffe with Mommy, she told me that was *nothing* at all."

Blushing, the father responds, "Aw shucks, son. Your mommy's just spoiled!"

THE SEX O'COCK NEWS is on the air!
Here's anchorman Bob Boner.

"Good evening, everyone. Today at the United Nations a major breakthrough in world affairs took place. Two major countries decided to unite: Ballswonia and Cocksylvania are now one nation. After being apart for so long they have tied the knot, so to speak. They wished to 'form a more perfect union,' in the words of an official spokesperson. We can all agree that the cocks and balls of the two formerly separate countries certainly do fit together well.

"Also here at home, Senator Rushhard admits he had misspoken during an address to the Family Values Coalition during its annual convention. 'I regret using the term *hard up for money'*, the senator laments. You can see in our taped segment how many mouths flew wide open and jaws dropped as the camera panned over the audience of attendees at the convention.

"With that, friends, we'll pause for a word from our sponsor and be right back with more news."

(**commercial**) Outdoor scene with a young girl running through a field of flowers. She stops and looks into the camera:

"Girls, do you ever need a fresh, feminine smell? That special scent of freedom throughout the entire day? Try our new and improved *Pussy Delight* for a hygienically clean, sensual and most alluring aroma ever! Available in aerosol spray, roll-on and powder at your favorite pharmacy or fancy goods dealer." Running off into the distance, the scene fades.

"Time once again for our world of sports. Here's Jack Shaft to fill you in on all of the latest stats and scores."

A lithe, prissy man dressed in a lavender double-breasted suit pinched at the waist and fluffing a paisley-print ascot with his limp wristed hand steps mincingly before the camera and begins to speak:

"Gee, thanks a bunch, darling Bob. Hi there, gang, how's it hanging? Jack Shaft here with the latest scoop for you sports fans out there! Today I've been invited to the annual Boys' Jockstrap and Pony Competition here at Fire Island. I simply must say that the young lads riding those sleek coated horseys would make the threads of any man's jockstrap snap noisily! Just look at them *cumming* out and *mounting* those steeds. My oh my, would I ever love to be horse whipped by one of those hunky jocks --- or

should I say, with a little giggle --- *jockettes*! See how they assemble at the starting line, waiting for the horn to signal that they're off. They're headed around the first bend, then the second, now the third and racing toward the finish line. The winner for this race is Hot Butts, and boy, does he ever have one --- shiny, too! I had the divine pleasure of interviewing the darling boy during my visit to the track."

(**inserted film segment**) "Hi there, cutie, and congratulations! How does it feel to be a wiener --- oopsie daisy, I mean, *winner*?"

"Well, Jack dear," the young handsome jockey gushes, "I can tell you that it's a real kick riding Hot Butts anytime."

"Ride 'em cowboy, as I always say, dearie! You know, sweetie, that I'll be in your dressing room later to examine that jockstrap of yours in order to give a detailed, accurate
report to all your fans out there in TV land. Whet our appetites a bit, stud muffin, and tell us what size do wear? It fits so incredibly snug and allows you to show off all your enormous assets, poopsie."

"I'm too embarrassed to say it aloud, Jack-Jack. Do you mind if I whisper it to you?"

Nodding, Jack Shaft leans toward the jockey's face with his ear cocked (no pun intended) and breaks out in tittery laughter as he listens.

"Oooh, you're such a silly thing, you! Back to you in the studio, Bob!" he chirps, wiggling his hand with an exaggerated flourish.

Wiping his brow and clearing his throat with embarrassment, Bob Boner exclaims, "Whew!

Thank goodness that's all from the world of sports for one broadcast. How can I possibly follow an act like that? The answer is simple: I can't, so we'll end today's newscast and hope you'll all tune in tomorrow when once again we present for your enjoyment and information the **SEX O'COCK NEWS**."

ROCK YOUR BALLS OFF

Now it's time for the overrated, X-rated ROCK YOUR BALLS OFF music show! Here's your swinging hosts on today's rockin' episode, none other than Horny and the Horndogs!

(***a young man with a crewcut, tight jeans and a black leather jacket struts onto the stage***)
"Hey, guys! Are ya ready to rock them balls and get yer rocks off? Here's our new hit song which is groping the Old Dong charts:

Hey, hey, hey, hey,
Ha, ha, ha, ha,
I wanna do it.
Hey, hey, hey, hey,
Ha, ha, ha, ha,
I wanna screw it.
And I wanna do with YOU!
Stroke, stroke, stroke,
You make me stroke it
While I'm screwing
And doing it
With YOU!
Ha, ha, ha, ha,
Pump, pump, pump, pump,
I'm pumping and
Screwing it
With YOU!

(*the music winds down, the STUDIO AUDIENCE applauds wildly and the lead singer takes a bow*)

(*offstage announcer*) Now let's hump the night away with The Hard Ones and their new hit single. It's called "In the Foreskin of the Night"

(*four gentlemen in blue suits take the stage and begin singing*)

In the foreskin of the night
Oh, how I love when you hold
And squeeze me tight,
Ba-ba-shoo-wah,
Oh, how I love when you pull it
And make me feel all right.
We can unravel the skin
All through the night
In the foreskin of the night.
Wah-wah-woo-woo-yeah.

(*announcer's voice offstage*) Thank you, gentlemen, for that rousing song. Now let's welcome those Drag Queens themselves as they offer us their smash hit from the latest chart-busting album. It's called, appropriately, "Trans Magic":
(*a group of elderly men gaudily dressed as women limp onto the stage*)

Oh, I love to dress up
at night
Love this girdle
But the dress
is too tight
It's Trans Magic
Doo-doo-doo-wah
Traaaa-ns Maaa-gic
Doo-doo-doo-wah
Oh, I love putting on makeup
To look trim and sexy
tonight

It's Trans Magic
Doo-doo-doo-wah
Traaaa-ns Maaa-gic
Doo-doo-doo-wah
It's really hot!
Traaaaaa-ns Maaaaa-gic
Doo-doo-doo-wah.
I'll show you what we've got!
It's all Trans Magic.
Traaaaaa-ns Maaaaa-gic
Doo-doo-wah-bam-boom!

(***finishing their song, the Drag Queens file offstage. One of them bends over in excruciating pain.***)

"Oh, hell! My damn arthritis is flaring up again, Agnes!" he shouts.

"Ernestine, you old hag!" Agnes scolds. "You're always complaining about something. You don't know what you want!"

"Shut up, you nasty bitch!" Ernestine snaps back. "Just because you're only 72 and healthier than I am is no reason to be mean like that."

"I'm sorry, dear," Agnes apologizes, laden with tears. "I don't know what gets into me at times. It must be that nerve tonic I've been taking."

(***the host hurries them along off the stage***). There they are, folks, the Drag Queens. And with special thanks also to the four Gentlemen in blue, better known as The Hard Ones and our own band, the Horndogs, this is Horny, hoping you'll all join us again to bust some nuts on our next show, right here on the overrated, X-rated **ROCK YOUR BALLS OFF** music show. Bye for now!

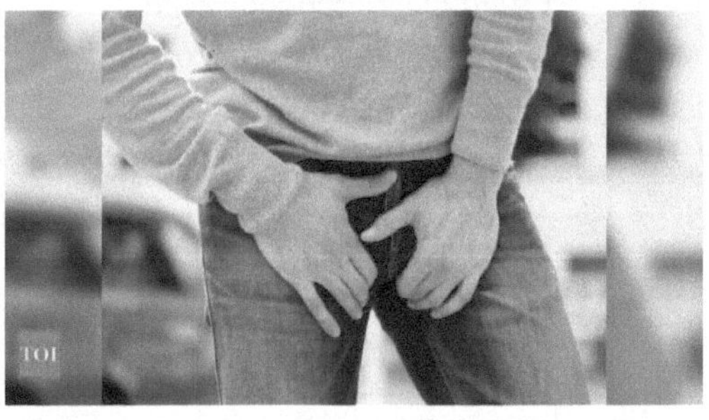

A new situation comedy
THE BOYS HAVE BALLS

Three high school boys loll around on the front porch of a suburban house.

"What're you planning to be when you graduate?" the first one asks.

"I wanna be a millionaire and own lotsa property," the second replies.

The third ponders the question and declares, "I wanna own me all them luxury cars I see parked down the street there."

Joey, the one asking the questions, turns scarlet red with embarrassment. "As for me, I've been thinkin' 'bout giving guys good blowjobs."

The other two look at him, raise their eyebrows and arch their bodies in an aggressive stance. "Whadya talkin' 'bout, idiot? Giving guys blowjobs?! Why'd ya wanna do that?"

Joey grins and answers, "My sister does that and she owns all them cars AND a whole bunch o' valuable property in town."

Shrugging, his friend Johnny quips, "Whatever... Ya know, it takes balls t' be guys like us."

"You're right about that, bro," the other buddy agrees. "There's one thing chicks ain't got."

"And what's that?"

Giving each other high fives, they shout in unison, "Balls!!"

"I got even with that nerdy teacher, Mister Jenkin. I nicknamed the guy 'Jerkington.' That old perv probably peeks into the boys' lockerroom to check out what goes on in the showers."

"Whad'ya do to get even with Jerkington?"

"I put a couple of tacks on his chair. That'll settle his ass down, but good!

The boys laugh in unison. David says, "That really takes balls."

"You got that right, man," Johnny proclaims. "I'm prouder than hell 'bout these nuts o' mine. I've got the wangingest, hangingest balls 'round these parts."

A new scene emerges. Bobby comes limping down the alley to get together with the rest of the guys. "What's wrong with you, Bob?" several of the boys ask.

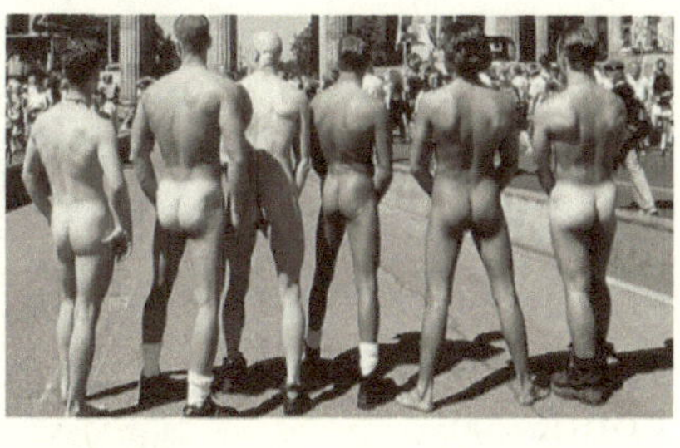

"Oh, I went up to the chick Nancy in my class and gave her a little pinch on the ass. She then turned and kicked me right in the nuts."

"You mean…?" the crowd of boys shudder.

"Yep," Bobby replies, "the balls. She's on a rampage now. Claims she hates all males and that all they're out for is to use her body." Scanning the distance, he adds, "Hey, she's headed this way now, gang. Better cover up your pride and joy if your value 'em."

Nancy reaches the end of the alleyway where the boys are huddled. "What a sorry looking group this is," she snickers. "Just stay where you are, smart asses, and don't make any sudden moves or I'll kick you in your…"

The boys interrupt her with a fury, completing her thought. "…BALLS!"

Nancy is so taken aback, she merely stands there and smiles from ear to ear.

THE HOUR OF BLESSINGS

Good day to you. I am the Reverend Anally Assnatious. I promote decency and preach against all naughtiness. I particularly find it appalling when they refer to me as "Your Ass-holiness."

I belong to the League of Anal Perversion Preservation. After all, one has been blessed with just one ass, not two, in this lifetime. So I ask you in all earnestness, why in the world would they invent a rubber dildo with two dickheads on it?

Our asses are such a blessed part of our bodies. Although I have heard the expression, "being a real asshole about it," I staunchly defend my position.

Now, dear friends, I have a special request: I would like each and every one of you to pull down your pants or lift up your dresses and gently place your ass cheeks on the TV screen. Have you done that? Good! I shall now chant a holy blessing upon all of your tushes.

O Divine Ass,
we ask you to bless
our royal asses,
protect and guide them

as we seek
your precious anal wisdom.
May all of our asses reach up and point to the heavenly skies.
O Great Ass Divinity,
I beg of you
to make proud asses
of us all.
Amen.

Get ready for an exciting, climaxing episode of everyone's favorite show, **TWO COCKS ARE BETTER THAN ONE**. The world's only two-headed dicks take on new adventures. Let's listen in:

One head turns to the other and asks, "Hey, Dicky, what're ya doin'?"

"Oh, just hangin' 'round, Pricky. I hear tell there are some real cool condoms they just came out with."

"Yep, I sure do enjoy the smooth kind. How 'bout you?"

"Ah, the lubricated kind're jus' as good. I hear you should be aware of the cheap kind, though."
"Yeah, Pecker Peter warned me 'bout that. He complained that one of them rubbers went flyin' clear 'cross the friggin' room."

"Why's that, son?"

"Oh, I think he was pissed off." Dicky and Pricky both break out into horse laughs.
"I've been a little hard up for dough lately," Pricky admits, putting on a sour face for Dicky.

"Bah! You're middle name is 'hard up,' ya dummy! You're always standing stiff at attention 'bout somethin'. If ya wanna know,

I've been havin' some problems performin' lately, if ya know what I mean. Can't get myself to stay up like before."

"Like the saying goes, man, 'the ol' grey prick ain't what it used to be.' What you need is some good blood circulation, baby."

"What circulation? My blood circulates just dandy!"

"Right. But it's all goin' to your damn head! No wonder you're so hard-headed 'bout things."

"They say through the shaft line that Pecker Peter caught himself a case o' the clap."

"My goodness! How the hell did that happen?"

"I can tell ya, goodness has nothin' to do wit' it.

The poor slob went to his doctor. The guy examined him and told him to cough. He damn near coughed himself into a grave."

Dicky and Pricky glance at one another, gasp and exclaim in unison, "Holy Peckeroonie!"

THE END

If you enjoyed this book, you might also like:

Available in paperback and Kindle formats

at

www.esmeraldalintner.net

and all Amazon sites worldwide

Simply search "ESMERALDA LINTNER"

www.ingramcontent.com/pod-product-compliance
Lightning Source LLC
LaVergne TN
LVHW040908150826
845672LV00007B/1941